EXPLORE SPACE!

EXPLORE ASTEROIDS

BY MARTHA LONDON

CONTENT CONSULTANT
SHERRY FIEBER-BEYER, PhD
ASSISTANT PROFESSOR
DIRECTOR OF UND OBSERVATORY
DEPARTMENT OF SPACE STUDIES
UNIVERSITY OF NORTH DAKOTA

Kids Core
An Imprint of Abdo Publishing
abdobooks.com

abdobooks.com

Published by Abdo Publishing, a division of ABDO, PO Box 398166, Minneapolis, Minnesota 55439. Copyright © 2022 by Abdo Consulting Group, Inc. International copyrights reserved in all countries. No part of this book may be reproduced in any form without written permission from the publisher. Kids Core™ is a trademark and logo of Abdo Publishing.

Printed in the United States of America, North Mankato, Minnesota
052021
092021

Cover Photo: QA International/Science Source
Interior Photos: Smilyk Pavel/Shutterstock Images, 4–5; JPL/NASA, 6, 10; Shutterstock Images, 7, 15, 20–21; Detlev van Ravenswaay/Science Source, 8; Michael Dunning/Science Source, 12–13; European Southern Observatory/Science Source, 17; JPL-Caltech/UCLA/MPS/DLR/IDA/NASA, 18; Andrzej Wojcicki/Science Source, 22; SETI/P/NASA, 23; Smithsonian Institution/Lockheed Corporation/NASA, 24; JPL-Caltech/ASU/NASA, 26; Safar Aslanov/Shutterstock Images, 28–29

Editor: Marie Pearson
Series Designer: Katharine Hale

Library of Congress Control Number: 2020948366

Publisher's Cataloging-in-Publication Data

Names: London, Martha, author.
Title: Explore asteroids / by Martha London
Description: Minneapolis, Minnesota : Abdo Publishing, 2022 | Series: Explore space! | Includes online resources and index.
Identifiers: ISBN 9781532195365 (lib. bdg.) | ISBN 9781644945407 (pbk.) | ISBN 9781098215675 (ebook)
Subjects: LCSH: Outer space--Exploration--Juvenile literature. | Asteroids--Juvenile literature. | Solar system--Juvenile literature. | Astrophysics--Juvenile literature. | Astronomy--Juvenile literature.
Classification: DDC 523.6--dc23

CONTENTS

CHAPTER 1
Coming Near Earth 4

CHAPTER 2
Our Solar System 12

CHAPTER 3
Tracking Asteroids 20

Space Notes 28
Glossary 30
Online Resources 31
Learn More 31
Index 32
About the Author 32

Scientists working at observatories study the asteroids in our solar system.

CHAPTER 1

COMING NEAR EARTH

It is April 2020. A scientist sits at her computer. She is tracking a big asteroid that is more than 1 mile (1.6 km) wide. The asteroid's name is 52768 (1998 OR2). It is going to pass close to Earth. But the scientist knows the asteroid will not hit Earth.

The Spitzer Space Telescope studied asteroids from 2003 until 2020.

Scientists track asteroids that could damage Earth if they hit the planet. Asteroid 52768 (1998 OR2) is one of those. The asteroid will fly even closer to Earth in 2079.

Telescopes showed images of the asteroid. It has a rough, gray surface. There are many hills and valleys. Smaller asteroids have hit it in the past. They made **craters** on its surface.

Asteroids come in many shapes and sizes.

Space Rocks

Asteroids are objects in space. They are made of metal, rock, or both. Sometimes they have ice on their surface. Asteroids are space rocks that are too small to be planets. Large objects have more **gravity** than smaller ones. Planets are big enough that their gravity pulls them into a round shape. Asteroids are not. They often have unusual shapes.

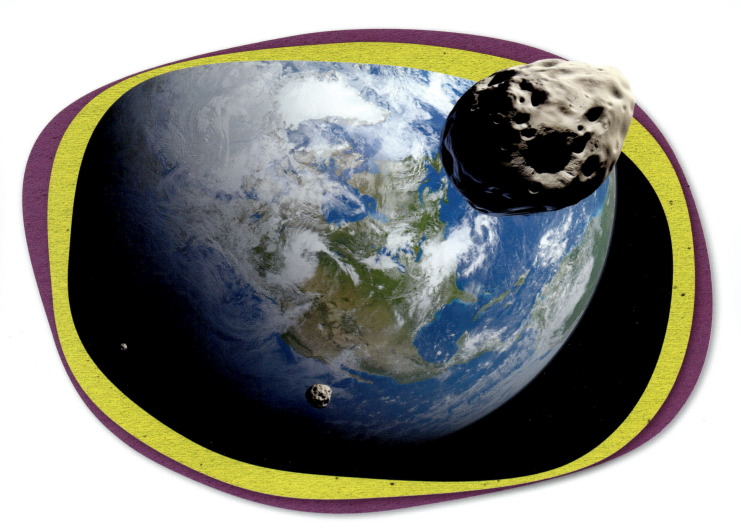

Most asteroids do not cause any damage to Earth.

Asteroids **orbit** the Sun. Some orbit the Sun close to Earth. Asteroids enter Earth's **atmosphere** every day. Most are small. When they hit the atmosphere, intense heat builds up.

The small asteroids burn up before they can hit the ground.

Giuseppe Piazzi was the first scientist to identify an asteroid. In 1801, he discovered the asteroid Ceres. Scientists continue to study Ceres and other space rocks.

Avoiding a Strike

Scientists study ways to keep large asteroids from hitting Earth. The best way to do that is to change an asteroid's orbit. Powerful magnets could push or pull an asteroid away. Strong explosions could also cause an asteroid to change its orbit.

The asteroid Ida is approximately 35 miles (56 km) in length.

NASA has a team that studies asteroids that could harm Earth. These scientists track the orbits of large space rocks. They work to protect Earth from asteroids. Scientists make sure large space rocks do not reach Earth's surface.

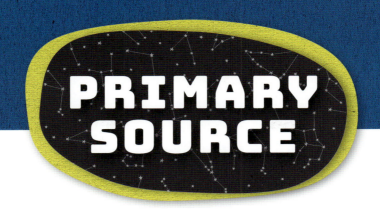

Scientist Flaviane Venditti explained that when asteroid 52768 (1998 OR2) gets closer, Earth might be at risk. Scientists can make a plan to protect Earth. She said:

> In 2079, asteroid 1998 OR2 will pass Earth about 3.5 times closer than it will this year, so it is important to know its orbit **precisely**.

Source: Andrew Griffin. "Mile-Wide Asteroid Set to Fly Near Earth." *Yahoo! News*, 27 Apr. 2020, yahoo.com. Accessed 28 May 2020.

Comparing Texts

Think about the quote. Does it support the information in this chapter? Or does it give a different perspective? Explain how in a few sentences.

Everything in the universe formed during the Big Bang.

CHAPTER 2

OUR SOLAR SYSTEM

There are many solar systems. Our solar system formed 4.6 billion years ago. It is younger than the age of the universe. The universe formed 13.8 billion years ago with a huge explosion. This explosion is known as the Big Bang.

Over time, gravity pulled dust and rocks together. Stars and planets formed. Some of them eventually became our solar system.

In our solar system, the first thing to form was the Sun, followed by the planets. The planets developed their own gravity. They pulled some objects toward them. Some of these objects became moons. Other rocks did not get pulled toward a planet. These rocks are asteroids. Asteroids are left over from the formation of the solar system.

The Belt

Most asteroids in the solar system are in an asteroid belt called the Main Belt. The Main Belt is located between Mars and Jupiter. These are

Main Belt

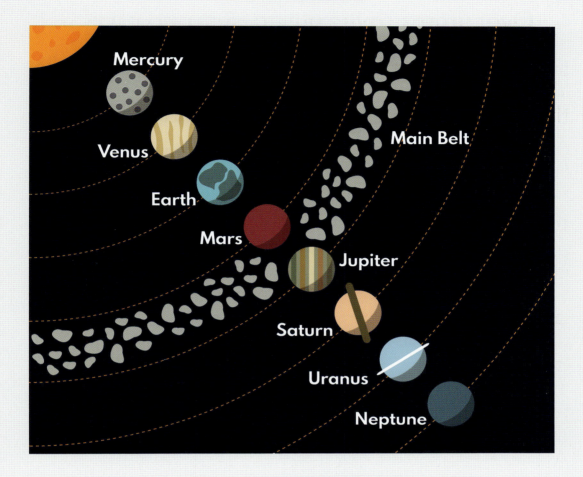

Most of the asteroids in our solar system are in the Main Belt between Mars and Jupiter.

the fourth and fifth planets from the Sun. But some asteroids exist closer to Earth or beyond Jupiter. Other solar systems have asteroids too.

Most asteroids have egg-shaped orbits. But some have circular orbits. Their orbits may take them very close to Earth. When an asteroid gets too close to Earth, it can get pulled out of its orbit. Earth's gravity pulls the asteroid toward the planet.

Space Rock Sizes

There are more than 1 million asteroids in the solar system. Some of these asteroids

Starlike Objects

Asteroid is a Greek word. It means "starlike." At first, scientist Giuseppe Piazzi thought there was a planet between Mars and Jupiter. But scientists soon realized they were seeing something smaller. Piazzi named this object Ceres.

A large asteroid may have smaller asteroids orbiting it.

are named after people. Asteroid 14825 Fieber-Beyer is named after scientist Sherry Fieber-Beyer. All asteroids have different shapes.

Some objects in the Main Belt, such as Ceres, are very large.

Asteroids can be many different sizes. Some are only a few feet across. These are also known as meteoroids. They are believed to be chunks broken off of larger asteroids. Others, such as Vesta, are hundreds of miles across. Ceres is even bigger than Vesta. It was called an asteroid for years. But in 2006, scientists decided Ceres was a **dwarf planet**.

Explore Online

Visit the website below. What new information did you learn about asteroids that wasn't in Chapter Two?

Asteroids

abdocorelibrary.com/explore -asteroids

Meteors falling to Earth are also called shooting stars.

CHAPTER 3

TRACKING ASTEROIDS

When asteroids enter Earth's atmosphere, scientists call them meteors. If a meteor hits Earth's surface, it is called a meteorite. Scientists track the orbits of large asteroids. If they hit Earth, these asteroids can cause a lot of damage.

The chances of a large asteroid hitting Earth are very low. But it would change life as we know it.

Large asteroids create huge explosions when they hit land or water. Scientists believe an asteroid hit Earth and killed almost all the dinosaurs 66 million years ago.

Scientists discovered pieces of rock from an SUV-sized asteroid in an African desert in 2008.

Large asteroids do not hit Earth very often. An asteroid the size of a car comes into Earth's atmosphere about once a year. It burns up before reaching Earth's surface. An asteroid would need to be more than 1 mile (1.6 km) wide to cause damage like the one that killed the dinosaurs. Those asteroids only come once every few million years.

The Hubble Space Telescope helps scientists learn about faraway asteroids.

Asteroids in the Night Sky

Most asteroids are too small and too far away to see with the human eye. Scientists use telescopes and **spacecraft** to study asteroids.

Telescopes make asteroids appear larger. Spacecraft take close-up photos of asteroids.

But people can sometimes see asteroids. Many small asteroids come into Earth's atmosphere every day and become meteors. They burn up. A burning meteor creates a bright tail. People can see these tails at night. They are called shooting stars.

Asteroids or Comets?

Like asteroids, comets orbit the Sun. However, they are made of different materials. Asteroids are made of rock, metal, or sometimes both. Comets are made of dust, rock, and ice. When a comet comes close to the Sun, the ice turns to gas and forms a tail behind it. People can sometimes see that tail when the Sun shines on it just right.

Scientists study asteroids such as Psyche in the Main Belt.

Asteroids are an important part of the solar system. They capture people's imaginations. They hold answers to how the universe began. Scientists continue to study asteroids. And people continue to look for them in the night sky.

Further Evidence

Look at the website below. Does it give any new evidence to support Chapter Three?

Asteroids

abdocorelibrary.com/explore -asteroids

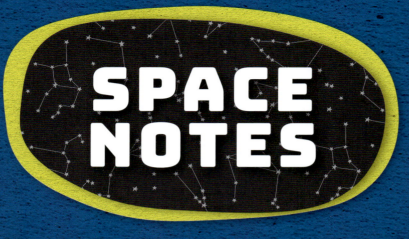

SPACE NOTES

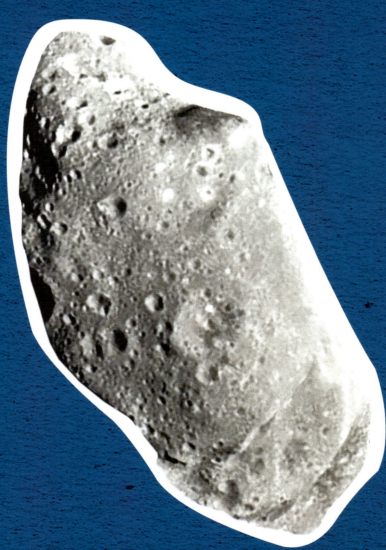

- Most asteroids in the solar system are in the Main Belt between Mars and Jupiter.
- Asteroids are the leftover rocks from when the solar system formed 4.6 billion years ago.

Lumpy Shape

Crater

Made of Rock and Metal

Glossary

atmosphere
a protective layer of gas around an object in space

craters
bowl-shaped features created in the ground by a falling object

dwarf planet
an object in space that is large enough that its gravity makes it round, but whose gravity isn't strong enough to clear its path of other objects

gravity
a force that pulls objects toward each other

orbit
to follow an oval-shaped path around a larger object

precisely
exactly

spacecraft
vehicles that can travel through space

Online Resources

To learn more about asteroids, visit our free resource websites below.

Visit **abdocorelibrary.com** or scan this QR code for free Common Core resources for teachers and students, including vetted activities, multimedia, and booklinks, for deeper subject comprehension.

Visit **abdobooklinks.com** or scan this QR code for free additional online weblinks for further learning. These links are routinely monitored and updated to provide the most current information available.

Learn More

DeYoe, Aaron. *Planets*. Abdo Publishing, 2016.

Kukla, Lauren. *Asteroids, Comets, and Meteoroids*. Abdo Publishing, 2017.

Murray, Julie. *Telescopes*. Abdo Publishing, 2020.

Index

atmosphere, 8, 21, 23, 25

Big Bang, 13

Ceres, 9, 16, 19
comets, 25
craters, 6

Fieber-Beyer, Sherry, 17
52768 (1998 OR2), 5–6, 11

gravity, 7, 14, 16

Jupiter, 14–15, 16

Main Belt, 14, 15
meteoroids, 19
meteors, 21, 25
moons, 14

orbit, 8, 9, 10, 11, 16, 21, 25

Piazzi, Giuseppe, 9, 16

Sun, 8, 14–15, 25

telescopes, 6, 24–25

Venditti, Flaviane, 11
Vesta, 19

About the Author

Martha London is a writer and educator. She lives in Minnesota and escapes to the woods whenever she can to look at the stars.